The jelly-like substance that surrounded the brain in the jar began to bubble a little.

"FARTHERMORE," the Head continued, "UNLOSS I SEE A MORKED IM-PROVEYMINT IN RESORTS, I SHAWL BE INTRODICING SATORDAY MORNINK SKULL!"

A horrified hush fell over the entire assembly. Miss Wagstaff swayed slightly and had to dip into her bag for smelling salts. Everyone was too stunned to take it in. Compulsory testing every day. And if marks didn't come up to scratch, Saturday morning school for all. It was too horrible for words.

THE REIGN OF TERROR

BLACK HOLE PRIMARY

4

Brough Girling and Damian Kelleher

Illustrated by
Robin Edmonds

Lions
An Imprint of HarperCollinsPublishers

First published in Great Britain in Lions in 1994

1 3 5 7 9 10 8 6 4 2

Lions is an imprint of HarperCollins Children's Books,
a division of HarperCollins Publishers Ltd,
77-85 Fulham Palace Road,
Hammersmith, London W6 8JB

ISBN 0 00 674714 0

Printed and bound in Great Britain
by HarperCollins Manufacturing Ltd, Glasgow

THE REIGN OF TERROR

CHAPTER ONE

Ben Gordon stood at the bus stop as he did every morning and checked his solar activated watch. 8:47 precisely. He looked to the top of Apollo 9 Avenue where his best friend Vernon lived, but there was still no sign of him. Ben checked his watch again. 8:48 now, and still no Vernon. Where was he?

At nine o'clock sharp, both Ben and Vernon were due to walk through the gates at Black Hole Primary, the school on the edge of the universe in Stratus B. It wasn't your average school, as you may know by now, but a rather odd mixture of earthlings, aliens and creatures from faraway planets. But the weirdest of all had to be the Head, who was just that. One great big brain sitting in a glass jar with the loudest voice in the cosmos. Yes, it was even louder than your mum's.

Ben was getting cross now. The bus was already late and he couldn't bear the idea of trying to set up another diversion to stall Grudge, the rusty old robot that drove the clapped out nuclear wreck each morning. It really was a dreadful banger, on its last wheels actually, and it wasn't exactly environmentally friendly either. Nuclear powered, it took many mega-gallons of zynthonium to get it going and even then it gave off huge clouds of evil smelling gases into the milky way. Ben's mother claimed she'd heard the Black Hole have a coughing fit once as the bus shuddered past.

The familiar wheezing noise of the bus's engine jolting through space caused Ben to check his watch again. 8:50 precisely, his watch said. That's it, thought Ben, I'm not holding the bus up today. Vernon will just have to space walk to school and make his own excuses.

As the bus approached the stop, the door opened and Grudge pressed the button marked "DROP ANCHOR". Ben took one last look towards Apollo 9 Avenue, and sure enough, the familiar shape of his best friend appeared, speeding around the corner, hanging on to his cap as he raced towards the school bus.

"Hold the bus, Ben!" he yelled.

Thinking fast, Ben dropped to his knees.

"What are you doing down there, you scheming little toe-nail," said Grudge from behind the wheel, lighting up another of his smelly old roll-ups. "Come on, get on, or I'm going without you. If I'm late again that barmy Miss Wagstaff'll do 'er nut."

"It's these new self-tying shoelaces," Ben lied. "I'm sure there's a problem with the microchip. Mine keep coming undone."

Ben looked towards Vernon who was now about a hundred metres away. Luckily, Vernon was the best sprinter in their class, Pulsar Remove, and moved like the clappers.

"You 'aven't even got laces on your blinking shoes, you rotten little fibber," coughed Grudge, squinting through the cigarette smoke at Ben's feet. "Right, you can make your own way. I'm off."

But by this time, Vernon had arrived and Ben hopped on smartly. He grabbed at Vernon's hand, yanking him up just as the auto-anchor (to stop the bus drifting off into another stratosphere) whizzed back up into the bus and the doors clanked shut.

Vernon held his hand up and Ben slapped his palm against it half-heartedly.

"Nice work, my man," smiled Vernon as he gasped for breath. "I knew I could count on you, Benny boy!"

As they passed through the bus, taking a seat behind a couple of dark Bourbons (half earthling, half biscuit), Ben spoke sharply to Vernon.

"Yes, well that's the last time, Vern.

Can't you get up earlier? We go through this same routine practically every day and I'm getting fed up with thinking up excuses to stall old grump features."

"Ooh, what's eating you, dude," said Vern. "Did you get out of the wrong side of your rest unit this morning?"

Ben looked at Vernon and a broad grin crossed his face. He wasn't the kind of boy that could stay angry for long.

"Actually, I couldn't wait to show you something," said Ben. "My mum came home with a surprise last night. Look!"

Ben searched around inside his school bag and produced two tickets. They had SPACE ASSOCIATION CUP FINAL ASTRON VILLA versus LUNARPOOL printed on the top in big letters.

"Wow! Jammy or what! Where did she get those? Your mum is something else, man, I tell you. Something else."

"Well, you know she works on the Black Hole patrol?" Ben explained proudly. Vernon nodded. Black Hole Patrol Wardens are a bit like traffic wardens, except that their job is to patrol the huge, ugly black hole from which the school gets its name, and to make sure that no one and nothing falls into it. "Well," continued Ben, "she happened to mention to this other warden, Bob Stroud, how I was the biggest Astron Villa fan in the universe…"

"Second biggest," Vernon corrected.

Ben smiled. "We"ll argue about that later. Anyway, it just so happens he had two tickets and wait for it - HE DOESN'T LIKE FOOTBALL!"

Vernon slapped his knee and cackled.

"UNBELIEVABLE! Who're you gonna take, Benny? Me, me, me!"

"I haven"t decided yet," Ben said, holding the tickets up to the light to check the watermark, and looking serious. "I know Gracie's quite keen on Lunarpool. I bet she'd like to go."

Vernon screwed up his nose and looked at Ben.

"You're kidding?"

"Course I am. It's you and me, Vern! We're up for the cup!"

Just as Ben and Vern burst into another bout of celebratory whoops, the bus gave out a long, low, death-rattle splutter. It rolled up just outside the school gates, took one last deep breath and died on the spot. Naturally, all the children burst out

laughing, and as they trooped off the ancient coach, a few of them pulled Grudge's cap down over his head and rang the bell, just to irritate him even more.

"Gerroff, urchins," Grudge rasped. "I 'ope you all 'ave some 'orribly 'ard sums today."

"Mr Grudge, I think your bus just died," said Ben, trying to keep a straight face as he approached the door.

"Nah, codsploppers," said Grudge. "It's fine. Just you listen to this."

The school caretaker-cum-chauffeur turned the key in the ignition and pumped his foot down hard on the accelerator. Nothing. He tried again. Still no response.

"When's the funeral, Grudge?" Vernon yelled as he jumped down.

"Come on," he said to Ben, "I'll race you through the gates!"

"Oh-oh," said Ben, looking at his watch again. "Do you realise what the date is today? April 1st - April Fool's Day, in other words. Do you think Grudge is trying to pull a fast one?"

"I don"t know about Grudge, but get a load of Doc Codger. Man, watch that cat go!"

Dr Codger, the school science master from the year dot, was speeding towards the gates on his bike like a Formula One racer. Tinkling his bell wildly, and yelling like a banshee, children scattered in all directions as he whizzed through the huge aluminium gates into the yard. He was heading for the school entrance, when who should suddenly step into his path but Miss Wagstaff, the Deputy Head and fashion teacher. Thinking quickly, Dr Codger steered his bike towards the rear of the school and disappeared round a corner at about a thousand kilometres an hour. Seconds later, there was a series of loud crashes followed by a dustbin lid that rolled out and finally came to rest at Miss Wagstaff's feet.

"Vernon, Ben, can you go and help Dr Codger out of Mrs Danvers' dustbins, please?" Miss Wagstaff sighed. Ridiculous old buffer, she thought. He's been teaching at this school for the best part of four centuries and he still doesn't know to check his brakes on April Fool's Day. Some people never learn.

As she turned to walk back into the school, the whole playground dissolved into laughter; pinned to the back of her brand new designer tapestry bolero jacket was a note that read, "JUMBLE SALE BARGAIN!"

CHAPTER TWO

Ben and Vernon's class was called Pulsar Remove, and their form teacher, Miss Calculate, was taking no chances. As she pressed the entry button to her class, she checked above the door to make sure that there were no flour bombs lurking on the corridor side. Looking left to right and back again, she stepped in smartly.

"Now before anyone decides to do anything silly, may I just remind you that I am quite aware of what day it is today, and I hope none of you is going to be foolish enough to try any silly tricks out on me." Miss Calculate was firm but fair, and popular with her pupils. Her subject was maths, and she looked just like a huge calculator and loved nothing better than getting to grips with some really riveting calculations.

"Roberta, would you like to come and remove this rubbish from my desk, please."

Roberta, the class bully, sulked her way to the front and grabbed at the empty fizzy drink can on Miss Calculate's desk. There was a loud bang, and Roberta squealed as her face turned completely black and her plaits stood out from her hair at strange angles. Everyone laughed.

"Yes, the old soot bomb in the drinks tin routine," Miss Calculate snorted. "I expected you to come up with something a little more original than that, Pulsar Remove. Roberta, you'd better go and wash your face."

Roberta walked over to the door and pressed the exit button. As the automatic door slid across, a large bag of flour fell off the top edge and dropped smack on to Roberta's head. Bullseye!

The class roared. Of course, all the traps had been set for the teachers, but getting Roberta was even more satisfying.

Roberta turned to face the rest of her class. She had turned from a black demon to a white witch in a matter of moments. Even her eyelashes were dropping flour as she snarled at them.

"Very funny, you pathetic bunch of nobodies! But just you remember this. Someone's going to pay for this, so you'd all better watch your backs. HEAR ME?!"

Roberta stomped out towards the chemical conveniences. Even Miss Calculate had to stop herself from smirking. Roberta's famous bully tactics were a common topic of conversation in the staffroom at Black Hole, and she was no more popular with the teachers than she was with the pupils.

"Serves her right for all the misery she's put us through," Gracie giggled to Ann

Droid, her robot friend who often suffered at the hands of Roberta's beastly bullying.

As soon as she had finished registration, Miss Calculate looked up at her pupils. A very difficult long division was feeding out of the side of her head, but Miss Calculate was saving that as a treat for herself - something to finish off at first break. She looked serious.

"The Head has an important announcement to make this morning," she warned her pupils. "Hurry along to assembly now, please. Don't dawdle and don't chat."

"I don't like the sound of this," said Ben to Gracie as they filed out of the class and on to the auto-walker. This was the automatic walkway that snaked around the entire school and sped teachers and pupils from one part of the huge educational complex to another.

"Me neither," agreed Gracie. "There's a storm brewing, I reckon."

"You don't think this has anything to do with Dr Codger's brakes this morning, do you?" asked Ann. "He could have had a nasty accident, you know."

"No way, man!" said Vernon. "Some

doofer pulls the same stunt every year with Doc Codger, so I guess you might say that he always falls for it!"

As everyone groaned at Vernon's joke, Miss Wagstaff pushed past them, speeding towards the corridor like a minor hurricane.

"Hurry along there, Pulsar Remove," she urged crossly. "We've a lot to get through this assembly. Chip-chop and cut the chat."

"She obviously found the note on her jacket," whispered Gracie to the others. "You don"t think that's what this is all about, do you?"

"GOOD MORNINK, PIPIPS!" The Head addressed the school in his usual loud bellow. Everyone had taken their places in the assembly hall and sat cross-legged on the floor, looking worried. You'd look worried too, if your Head teacher looked more like an under-poached egg in a glass jar and had to be wheeled around on a high-tech supermarket trolley, speaking via two loud-speakers attached to him with wires and pipes and tubes. Yuk!

"I HAVE A VERY IMPORTIP ANNOUNCEABUBBLE TO MIKE ."

"Here we go," whispered Ben to Vernon.

"IT HAS COMET TO MY NOTICE THAT CERTAIN PARENTALS AND THE INTERGALACTIC MINISTRY OF EDUCATION ARE COMPLAINITIOUS ABOUT STANDODDLES OF TORCHING AT MY SCHOOL."

"What *is* he talking about?" Ann asked Vernon.

"He says Black Hole ain't up to scratch," Vernon translated.

"AS A DIROCT RESULTIP, I HAVE DEDIDUOUD TO INTROBURB COMPILSORY TOASTING IN ALL SOBJICTS. I MY SLOATH WILL REVERSE ALL FONDANTS."

Ann turned to Vernon again.

"He's introducing compulsory tests," Vernon explained glumly. "And he's going to review all the results himself. What's the matter with you, Ann? Can't you speak plain English?"

"*I* can," remarked Ann defensively. "Trouble is, the Head can't!"

"FARTHERMORE," the Head continued, "UNLOSS I SEE A MORKED IMPROVEYMINT IN RESORTS, I SHAWL BE INTRODICING SATORDAY

21

MORNINK SKULL!"

A horrified hush fell over the entire assembly. Not even Ann needed that last bit translated. Saturday morning school! The very idea had rocked the assembly to its foundations.

Miss Wagstaff was obviously as shocked as everyone else. She swayed slightly and had to dip into her bag for smelling salts. Taking a good strong snort, she opened her eyes as wide as saucepan lids, shook her head and took a deep breath.

"Are you all right, ding-a-dong?" Orchestra, the music teacher, asked her in her usual sing-song voice. "You look a little faint, Miss Wagstaff, tra-la-la."

"Oh, I'm fine," said Miss Wagstaff, obviously close to tears. "I just wish the Head would consult me a little more. This is the first I knew of this ridiculous Saturday morning school notion."

"DOZE ANYBUBBLE HOVE ANY QUESTIOPLES?" asked the Head.

Nobody answered. Everyone was still far too stunned to take it all in. Compulsory testing every day. And if marks didn't come up to scratch, Saturday morning school for all. It was too horrible for words. Suddenly, one hand shot up.

"You have a question from the floor, sir," Miss Wagstaff prompted the Head.

"STAND IP, STOAT YOUR GNOME AND CLUSS AND OSK YOU QUESTIOPLE," roared the Head.

"My name is Ben Gordon and I'm form monitor in Pulsar Remove," Ben declared bravely, his voice quavering a little with nerves. "I'd like to know when exactly Saturday morning school is due to start if we don't pass our tests."

The jelly-like substance that surrounded the brain in the jar began to bubble a little, a sure sign that the Head was becoming agitated.

"Why do you ask that, man?" whispered Vernon. "He don't look one happy dude. I reckon that brain is like a volcano on the blink!"

"I asked because the match is on Saturday," hissed Ben. "The highlight of my life up until now and we've got tickets, remember. I can't miss that, Vern, I can't!"

The jelly around the Head slowly began to settle again.

"TOASTING WILL BE INTRODUCTED IMMEDIOPLE," announced the Head, "OND IF RESULTIPS ARE NOT SATISFACTYFICTION, SATORDAY MORNINK SKULL WILL BEGAN THIS WAKE."

Vernon looked at Ben in dismay.

"Oh, man," he whispered, "I'm beginning to wish you hadn't asked!"

CHAPTER THREE

As Miss Calculate walked out of the staff-room and was about to step on to the auto-walker to go to her first lesson of the day, she was intercepted by Miss Wagstaff.

"Oh, Miss Calculate, I need a word with you."

"Yes?" said the maths teacher, a little impatiently.

"Have you got Pulsar Remove next?"

"Yes, unfortunately."

"Well, look, I'm sorry about this, but the Head has just given me this." It was a thick sheaf of computer printout paper, bound down one side with a large black plastic strip.

"It's from the Ministry of Intergalactic Education, part of the new Cosmic Curriculum, apparently. The Head says you've got to put it into effect immediately.

He's pretty steamed up about it…"

Miss Calculate looked down at the first page of the document. RATS, it said. She looked again, but before she had read anything, Miss Wagstaff said something that sent a nasty tingle down Miss Calculate's electromagnetic spine.

"Apparently it's a form of New Maths. RATS stands for Rigorous Arithmetic Testing System. The Head says that if Pulsar Remove don't pass all the tests, they'll be here every Saturday for the next hundred light years. I'm truly sorry."

Miss Calculate could see that Miss Wagstaff meant it.

"I'm afraid we're at the start of a reign of terror at Black Hole," said the Deputy Head. "Everything's gone testing crazy. Teaching isn't the caring, rewarding profession that it used to be."

Miss Calculate took the large document, sighed, and set off down the corridor on the auto-walker. When she arrived at the entrance hatch of Pulsar Remove's classroom she checked the top of it for soot or flour, and stepped inside. She carefully removed the upturned drawing pin from the teacher's stool, and sat down.

"The jokes stop here, Pulsar," she said. "Turn on your screens."

The class all turned on their monitors.

"You know what the Head said about new standards? Well, they start right now."

She opened the printout and tapped at the keys on the Central Miniframe Processing Console Unit on the teacher's desk. "You'll see a maths problem coming up on your screens. Start working on it. When you've got the answer, enter it and press next on your keyboards. According to this new directive from the Ministry, there are sixty-seven problems to be worked through. Anyone getting less than seventy-five per cent right will have failed the RAT - that's a Rigorous Arithmetic Test - and according to the Head's new ruling, the whole class will then have to report for school at 8.45 this Saturday."

The pupils of Pulsar Remove could tell from the way she was speaking that Miss Calculate, usually a cheerful and popular teacher, was not happy. Her voice had that flat, dull tone, like a robot's when its battery pack is on the way out.

"Hey man," whispered Vernon. "I don't like the sound of this. No way man."

He, Ben, Gracie and Ann Droid were hunched around a monitor near the back of the class (there were never enough screens to go round at Black Hole). They stared in horror as a sum flickered up on the small blue screen:

A space rocket X with a velocity coefficient of 70.26 Miles per Light Year leaves Jupiter at 5.09 hours Galactic Mean Time (Use 57/3452 x 12.9, T - z to calculate local time). It travels towards Mars. Rocket Y leaves Mars at datum 70.9, travelling at 7.5 times the speed of rocket X, minus an Adiabatic Lapse Rate of a-.7920. Given magnetic variance of 24,976823K, and an orbital correction of Y-4256Px7, and assuming that it's not raining calculate, to the nearest millisecond, when the two vehicles will cross. Give your answer in both Lunar and Nebular time.

Ben looked at Vernon. Vernon looked at Ben.

"Who do they think we are, man, Einstein?" hissed Vernon.

"I couldn't do that sum if it meant Space Cup Final tickets every year for the next millenium," agreed Ben.

"Please Miss," said Vernon, putting up his hand.

"Yes, Vernon?" answered Miss Calculate rather crisply. "What is it?"

"Please Miss. If we can't do the first sum Miss, what should we do?"

"Well, maybe you should try the second one. Don't forget though, that you've got to get seventy-five per cent right. I trust you have some idea what seventy-five per cent means?"

"Oh yes, Miss Calculate," replied

Vernon, and he pressed enter and next on the keyboard.

The screen responded:

If it takes 5 space labour operatives 7.62 stellar hours to dig a trench 1.89 metres deep along the entire length of latitiude 56 degrees on Neptune, calculate how long 14.75 operatives would take to dig a trench three times as deep round the equator on Mars (conversion coefficient X - 4827593.897P squared) given that they start on the first day of gallactic leap year 1957, and that Thursdays are early closing (and 1st May is a Bank Holiday).

Ben and Vernon exchanged looks again.

"Gracie?" said Ann Droid to her special friend.

"Yes?" said Gracie.

"Gracie, I think I just might be going to have one of my systems overloads," said Ann Droid.

Vernon, Ben, and the rest of Pulsar Remove knew how she felt.

CHAPTER FOUR

"I don't believe this," said Ben despairingly. "This morning I was the happiest earthling in the Cosmos, bar none. And by first break, I've nothing left to live for."

The crew from Pulsar Remove had gathered round at their usual spot, near the perimeter fence of the Black Hole, to discuss the morning's events. A large cloud seemed to hang over the assembled throng - and Ben and Vernon in particular.

"Honestly, you do exaggerate, Ben," said Ann sensibly. "It is only a football match after all. Worse things have been known to happen, you know."

"Worse things! Worse things!" spluttered Vernon. "What could be worse than missing the greatest team in the universe enjoying their finest hour, huh?"

"It is only a game you know," chipped in

Gracie. "There are other things in life besides football."

"Like what?" moaned Ben, holding up his tickets and looking at them with tears in his eyes. "If I don't get to the match on Saturday, I might as well go and jump in the Black Hole."

"Oh please, what a pathetic little bunch you are!" Roberta stood in front of everyone with one hand on her hip. Her hair still had some tell-tale traces of flour in it, and if you looked closely you could still see a little sooty powder resting on her eyelashes.

"You should listen to yourself some time, Ben Gordon," she continued, spitting at him with her acid tongue. "Can't you think of anything more interesting to talk about than twenty-two grown men kicking a silly little object around a field for half an hour."

"Ninety minutes, actually," corrected Robbie, Roberta's weedy twin brother .

Roberta twisted around sharply.

"That's enough from you," she spluttered. "I've already been humiliated once today, without backchat from an insolent little tike like you. You're about as

32

much use as a perforated nappy!"

Robbie hung his head quietly. He was no match for his bully of a sister when she was in one of these moods.

"Let me look at those precious tickets a moment," Roberta sneered with a wicked smirk on her face. She snatched Ben's tickets from his hand and fanned herself with them. Everyone had noticed the devilish glint in her eye. Roberta was in a dangerous mood.

"Give me those back, please Roberta," Ben said slowly, holding out his hand towards her. "They're not yours, they're mine."

"Oh, soon changed your tune, haven't you," laughed Roberta. "One minute ago, you were moaning on about never getting to your precious match, and now it seems you haven't given up hope after all."

"Just give him back the tickets, all right?" Vernon looked nervously at Roberta as he spoke. "I don't know what you're panicking for," she hissed at Vernon. "Didn't you hear the Head's little speech this morning? With compulsory testing introduced this week, we'll all be back in this dump on Saturday anyway."

"I don't like this sort of thing," Ann whispered to Gracie. "This is turning into another one of Roberta's ugly strops. Why can't she just be pleasant for once?"

"I don't suppose it's in her nature," Gracie whispered back. "Are you OK, Ann? You look a bit peculiar. You don't feel an overload coming on, do you?"

Poor Ann Droid often suffered system overloads when she was feeling upset or under stress. She couldn't bear scenes.

"I'll tell you what, Ben-smarty-pants,"

Roberta continued, still waving the tickets around. "I've had a cracking idea. I'll hang on to these tickets, but I'll issue a little challenge to you all. Whoever comes up with a corking April Fool trick wins the rotten tickets!"

"But they're mine anyway," Ben pointed out reasonably enough. "You can't do that."

"Oh, can't I?" snarled Roberta. "I warned you lot this morning that someone would have to pay for making me look a total blimp in front of the whole class! Well you'll do, Ben Gordon! You should thank me for being so generous and giving you the chance to win your miserable tickets back!"

"An April Fool idea?" said Gracie, trying to get the challenge clear in her mind.

"That's right! You heard me," Roberta snapped back. "And it had better be something good and original. Better than the snivelling soot in the can and flour bomb tricks you lot came up with this morning!"

"I'll come up with something, don't worry," Ben said, with determination in his voice.

"Well don't be all year about it,"

Roberta continued. "You've only got until the end of today."

"And what happens if we haven't come up with a good enough idea by the end of today?" asked Hector Vector, a small green alien.

"Oh, I'm glad you asked me that, Hector," said Roberta. "If no one has come up with a really good" – and she looked around at them all grimly – "and I mean a REALLY good idea by the end of today, I may just lose my grip on these tickets, and you know what that means, don't you?"

"No," said Ann very quietly. "What does it mean?" She was quite close to tears now. She knew how much those tickets meant to Ben. How dare Roberta! How dare she!

"It means, you rusty lump of space junk," continued Roberta, "that they might just drift off into the Black Hole."

Roberta waved her hands in the direction of the huge gaping space that dominated the horizon. She let out a high-pitched giggle of delight and clasped a hand over her mouth in mock dismay.

"I say! Wouldn't that be awful, chaps!" With a dreadful smirk, Roberta turned and

sauntered off in the direction of the classroom.

"Do you think she's bluffing?" Ben asked the others as soon as Roberta was out of earshot.

"She was *really* mad this morning," Robbie pointed out.

"She had that crazy look on her face," said Gracie. "I think she's serious."

"Me too," said Vernon. "I reckon it's time to get our thinking caps on, dudes. Roberta's not fooling - she means business!"

CHAPTER FIVE

We don't know if you've ever been in the Black Hole Primary kitchens before, but sorry, we've got to take you there now.

Mrs Danvers, possibly the worst school cook in the history of cosmic catering, was up to her massive elbows in steamy cooking. She'd peeled nearly half a ton of turnips, and now had them boiling to death on her large nuclear-powered cauldron. She was busily dipping slices of old liver into a large bucket of grey batter, when her old friend and companion Mr Grudge clanked in.

"Howayer doin', Mrs D?" he asked.

"Terrible, as usual!" she replied wiping her large forearm across her damp nose with a deep sniff. "Bloomin' dinners, bloomin' school!"

"Don't talk to me about bloomin'

38

school!" said Grudge, sitting down carefully on a relatively clean patch of the kitchen table. "You should see that blinking bus they make me drive. It packed up completely this morning."

"What's wrong with it then?" asked Mrs Danvers.

"I dunno... I'm an odd-job robot, not a bloomin' space rocket mechanic. All I know is it's clapped out. Yesterday I tried to pull away from the lights on the corner of Quasar Avenue and Interstellar Drive - near the Apollo cinema, and I got overtaken by a dog with a wooden leg!"

They both cackled with laughter at

Grudge's little joke.

"The gearbox is up the spout, I reckon," he added. "It won't go at all now. With a bit of luck all the kids are going to have to walk home from school today!"

"Serve 'em right!" said Mrs Danvers with a sneer. "Spoilt little creeps. We didn't even have a school bus when I was a girl. I lived on the planet Ulcer Major, out beyond Stratus D. We used to walk miles. Never worried us. All kids do these days is sit about filling their fat faces with sweets."

"Yeah," agreed Grudge. "And watching tele-viewers and playing them stupid total reality video games."

"In them days my dad didn't even have a car," said Mrs Danvers, wistfully.

"No, but I bet your mum had a broomstick!" They cackled with laughter again. Mrs Danvers had a soft spot for Grudge, and didn't mind when he teased her.

Just then Miss Wagstaff walked into the kitchen. Mrs Danvers did *not* have a soft spot for Miss Wagstaff, in fact she regarded her as the universe's busiest busybody.

"Eee up!" sneered the school cook. "Here comes the biggest mouth this side of the Milky Way!"

Miss Wagstaff pretended she hadn't heard this comment.

"Mrs Danvers, I'm sorry to interrupt your cooking…" Mrs Danvers' eyes opened wide with surprise. She had never heard Miss Wagstaff being polite before. "But I'm afraid that the Head has had some instructions from the Ministry."

"Oh yeah?"

"Yes, and he's certainly taken them to heart. It means a whole new regime at Black Hole. The children are being tested in absolutely everything, and there's a request for new, higher standards in teaching and general behaviour."

"So what?" said Mrs Danvers, fearing that Miss Wagstaff had not yet got to the main point.

"Well, as I said, the Head is demanding higher standards in *every* aspect of school life. That means school food's got to improve as well."

"IMPROVE!? HOW ON URANUS COULD THE FOOD IMPROVE!?"

Mrs Danvers was turning an angry shade of purple, in fact her face was now the colour of a fresh bruise. "Look here Miss Bossy-Bum Wagstaff! I slaves my guts out in this here kitchen! And I does it on a budget!"

"She does an' all," chipped in Grudge, in a gesture of solidarity.

"I gives the kids here a high protein diet that's rich in fibre and trace elements! They gets lots of lovely liver and yesterday they had proper cabbage for veg. Just what are you on about?"

"It's nothing to do with me, Mrs Danvers, it's a directive from the Head. If you think you've got problems, think of the poor little children. They have got to pass attainment targets in absolutely everything, or come back to school on Saturday morning."

"Poor little children my backside!" snarled the cook. "If I had my way they'd have raw potato and a thick ear each for dinner!"

"Look," said Miss Wagstaff trying to stay calm. "Couldn't you make just a teeny, weeny effort, otherwise I'm afraid it'll be the Head who'll be speaking to you direct..."

Mrs Danvers gave a small shudder. (Like all bullies she was quite afraid of being bullied herself.)

"I know," continued Miss Wagstaff. "Why don't you try adding a little something special to lunch today. That would impress him."

"Like what?" said Mrs Danvers sulkily.

"Like a bit of gravy, perhaps?"

"GRAVY?! I've never made gravy in my life! We never had no gravy on Ulcer Major when I was a girl. What do kids want with gravy?"

"Well actually, they rather like it, and it might help the liver go down." Miss Wagstaff almost gagged at the thought of Mrs Danvers' liver but managed not to show it. "I'm afraid that if you don't, the

Head is likely to start advertising for a new school cook. He's in a *very* determined state of mind."

Reckoning that she'd got her message across, Miss Wagstaff smiled a sweet and not very sincere smile and left the room.

"Gravy!" said Mrs Danvers with a snarl as the door closed. "That's the last straw, that is."

"Quite right, Mrs D," agreed Grudge. "As a robot, I don't actually have to eat, but I never could see no sense in things like gravy. Poncy food if you ask me!"

"Poncy food for a poncy school!" said Mrs Danvers. She took a massive saucepan from a rack above the sink. "It"s one thing after another in this place. They'll want custard with their boiled lard puddings next!"

"I must say I wouldn't want your job, Mrs D," said Grudge. "At least the Head leaves me in peace. Once I've done my bus run I can hide down in the boiler room and put my feet up for the rest of the day!"

Unfortunatley, Miss Wagstaff returned at this point and put her head round the kitchen door.

"Oh, by the way, Mr Grudge," she said.

"The Head says that the school bus is a total disgrace and not up to the new school standards required by the Ministry. He wants it serviced, washed, polished and in good working order by the end of school today. Thank you."

CHAPTER SIX

"Come on you lot, keep the queue moving," Mrs Danvers hollered at the top of her voice while she absent-mindedly scratched the tattoo on her left bicep. "This isn't a holiday camp, you know."

She dipped a massive great spoon into a huge vat of greasy-looking rubberised craters and dropped one savagely on to the plate of the next Black Hole pupil who filed past. It was Robbie, who looked down at the object with a mixture of amusement and horror. It lay there, unmoving and disgusting.

"Please Mrs Danvers, what is it?" Robbie asked politely.

In a trice, Mrs Danvers had grabbed Robbie by his collar and tie, and yanked him across the counter.

"Don't get funny with me, sonny," she screeched. "I'll have you know that crowned heads of Europe have come up for second helpings of my liver fritters."

"She must mean Marie Antoinette," Ben giggled to Gracie.

"After she had had her head chopped off!" Gracie whispered back.

"One of the world's greatest poets once wrote me a few lines inspired by my liver fritters," Mrs Danvers continued.

"I bet I know what those lines were," Vernon told Ann. "I MUST REMEMBER NEVER TO EAT MRS DANVERS' LIVER FRITTERS AGAIN."

The school cook suddenly decided she had strangled Robbie for long enough. Letting go quickly, he fell sprawling to the floor, coughing wildly.

"That'll teach you to make fun of my cooking, young fellow me lad," she snapped, and whacked the next fritter on to Gracie's plate with such vigour that the plate cracked in two.

The dinner lady standing next to Mrs Danvers looked like an all-in wrestler. She wore thick bovver boots and a dirty old donkey jacket with HELL'S DINNER LADIES crocheted on the back. Sniffing loudly, she leant over to Gracie and enquired in a deep voice, "Gravy?"

Gracie was petrified. Her nose warned her off the gravy, but her better instincts told her to accept the offer. A refusal could offend, Gracie decided.

"Thank you," she whispered hoarsely, and then added, as the congealed liquid fell off the ladle in lumps, "it looks very nice."

Mrs Danvers whispered into the dinner lady's ear: "That's the way, Audrey. Intimidate 'em into taking it, the crafty little so-and-so's."

Just as the pupils from Pulsar Remove were taking their seats, Miss Wagstaff appeared, wheeling the Head's trolley in front of her.

"Oh, we are privileged," Ann announced to the others. "I can't remember the last time the Head turned up in the lunch hall."

"Or Miss Wagstaff for that matter," said Gracie. Miss Wagstaff always tried her level best to avoid Mrs Danvers' domain if she possibly could. It was the smell she disliked more than anything else. She was trying to hold a lace hanky to her nose with one hand whilst steering the Head's trolley with the other, but she was fighting a losing battle. Some days, the smell of Mrs Danvers' cooking could reach as far as Pluto.

Miss Wagstaff took her hanky away from her nose for a minute, took a deep breath and began to speak.

"Would you all lay down your knives, forks, chopsticks…"

"…pneumatic drills, chisels," Vernon chipped in.

"…and other feeding utensils, please," said Miss Wagstaff. "The Head has a rather serious announcement to make." She turned to the brain in the jar on the trolley and said in a low voice, "The stage is yours, Head."

"MAY I REMAND YOU ALL THAT FROM TIDAY LEFTYOVERS ARE BUNNED," the bossy brain in the bell jar boomed out. "THERE WILL BE NO

49

SCRAPS OF ANY FORM LEFT ON ANY PLOTS, UNDERSTOOD? YOU ARE TO OAT EVERYTHING, AND DON'T THINK YOU KEN SMOGGLE IT OUT BECAUSE MRS DINVERS WILL BE SORCHING ALL PICKETS AND BUGS PERSONILLY."

Mrs Danvers stepped up behind the Head. She was pounding a ladle into her open hand repeatedly in a very threatening manner. Ann began to shake.

"I don't think I like this school any more," she whispered to Gracie.

"You're not the only one," Gracie replied. "I'd rather eat my mum's cooking than Mrs Danvers' and that's fairly disgusting too!"

At that moment, an infant approached the rack of empty trays where the dirty plates were stored. Mrs Danvers pounced.

"Look at this shocking waste, Head," she wailed. "Three peas left on this plate and a good spoonful of my lovely gravy. Ooh, it's wicked it is, sir! Wicked!"

The young Venusian in question looked as though he was about to burst into tears.

"TICK IT BUCK TO YOUR SEAT AND FAMISH IT UP," the Head decreed.

"I WILL NOT TULERITE THIS OVAL WASTAGE, DO YOU HARE ME? I GIVE MRS DINVERS MY PREMISSION TO PUT ANY FOOD WISTERS INTO CUSTARD AND JELLY, OVERSTOOD?"

"No, I don't understand him at all," Ann said to Ben, as Miss Wagstaff and the Head made a hasty exit. "What was that all about?"

"He's giving Mrs Danvers the power to take us into custody if we don't finish our meals," Ben explained.

51

"Man, I don't believe that guy," Vernon moaned, sweeping his hand through his hair in an act of desperation. "This place becomes more like a prison every day!"

As the gang sat down to their lunch, a grey cloud of gloom seemed to hang over everyone. Even Ann, who normally managed to keep cheerful, looked a complete misery.

"There's something moving underneath your lettuce," Ben pointed out to Gracie as she took a sip from her drink of astro milk.

"Are you sure?" Gracie replied suspiciouly, wiping away her milky moustache. "This lettuce looks about as dead as the school bus to me."

"Honest. I saw it move," Ben answered. "Look, there. It just jumped!"

"Crumbling craters, so it did," giggled Gracie. Slowly, she stretched out her hand and picked up the lettuce leaf. Underneath it sat a multi-coloured frog (the sort you only find in tropical rainforests and the deserts of Jupiter).

"OK, I know it's April Fool's Day, but who is responsible for this?" Gracie demanded. The rest of the children burst into huge peals of laughter, Vernon guffawing even louder than the rest.

Unfortunately, he then took a huge forkful of potato from his plate and spat it back out again immediately.

"Ugh, gross, man, that is DISGUSTING! This mash is as hard as rock."

It was Gracie's turn to laugh until the tears rolled down her face.

"OK, Gracie, nice trick," Vernon acknowledged. "What was it?"

"Oh just a little butter, milk, a twist of black pepper and quite a lot of plaster of Paris," Gracie sniggered. "And don't forget to clear your plate Vern, or you'll have Mrs Danvers locking you up!" she added.

"When you've quite finished, perhaps you'd like to put the roof back on my house please," the multi-coloured frog said, looking at Gracie.

"Wow, a talking frog," Ann sighed in wonder. "Now that's what I call a good April Fool."

"Do you mind?" said the frog, crossly. "I'm a rare talking tree-frog from the arid wastelands of Jupiter. When you've quite finished gawping at me, perhaps I could get some kip. April fool, indeed - blooming cheek," he muttered, as he pulled the lettuce leaf over his head and went to sleep.

CHAPTER SEVEN

"Gracie! Quick!" said Ben, his voice full of urgency.

"What's up?" said Gracie.

"It's Ann! Take a look at her."

Gracie, the ace electronics expert of Pulsar Remove, took a look at Ann Droid, and instantly saw what Ben was worried about. Ann's face had turned pale, and her eyes were swivelling alarmingly.

"Oh-oh! It's a systems overload all right," said Gracie. "Quick, help me get her control panel off. If we're not sharp about it, her random memory banks will wipe, and the hospital will have a major reprogramming job on its hands! Vernon, go and get my schoolbag from my desk, it's got my tools in it. Hurry!"

Just then, however, several infants gave a yell from the other side of the dining hall and Ben looked up to see a small pink piglet run under their table.

"What on earth is going on?" shouted Dr Codger, who was sitting on a staff table nearby.

"It's not on earth, Dr Codger," quipped Mr Stretch, the PE teacher. "It's under the table!"

Miss Fluffety, the nice lady who taught the Black Hole infants, stood up on her chair and screamed. She was usually very gentle and quiet, so this was the loudest noise anyone in the school had ever heard her make.

Miss Wagstaff screamed too: "Help! There's a pig in the dining hall!"

"Don't worry. I'll deal with this," announced Mr Stretch. He rather fancied Miss Wagstaff, and here was a good opportunity to impress her with some bravery, athleticism and general heroics.

He dived at the pig, sending a bench full of infants and several glasses of water flying.

"I've got it!" he shouted, and he emerged from the table holding the struggling piglet in his arms.

The next minute, the piglet was free again, having bitten Mr Stretch on the chin.

"Oh no!" exclaimed the PE teacher.

"Someone's covered the thing in grease - it's as slippery as an eel in washing-up liquid!"

He was right. Someone had released a greased piglet into the school dining hall.

Ben, Gracie and several of their friends looked at each another in amazement. "As if Ann's systems overload wasn't enough to cope with!" said Gracie urgently. "I wish Vernon would hurry up with my tool kit!"

Ben glanced at Ann Droid. Her eyes had stopped swivelling now and were closed. She appeared to be semi-conscious.

The piglet was conscious enough, though.

Mr Stretch had managed to regain a hold on one of its back legs, but that wasn't stopping the pig from dragging him round and round the hall, squealing like a banshee with a belly ache.

Vernon arrived, and stepping over a couple of fallen infants, he plonked Gracie's schoolbag on the table in front of her.

"Right, guys," said Gracie, "I may need your help."

In a trice she'd got the inspection hatch off Ann's back, and was peering inside, parting a forest of wires and circuit boards with a long red-handled screwdriver.

"Oh-oh," she said, her brow furrowed.

"This is a bit more than a simple overload. The girl's in a bad way this time."

The pig, still pursued by Mr Stretch, knocked Miss Fluffety off her chair and into the remains of several half-eaten liver dinners.

"It's the main bearing on her central systems bank hard disc drive..." said Gracie, still peering deep into Ann's inner workings. I can change her ROM supplementary circuit boards, but that drive is something else. It's in danger of total mechanical breakdown."

The pig bit Dr Codger on the back of the leg, and both of them yelled.

"I think it needs some sort of high-tech heavy duty industrial lubricant," said Gracie.

Then her face lit up with a smile. "Ben, be so good as to pass me your plate, would you."

"You what?" said Ben, puzzled, as the pig up-ended Miss Wagstaff. But Ben slid his uneaten plate of the universe's greasiest and most revolting food towards her.

As the piglet did something too smelly and terrible to tell you about in the corner of the room, Gracie dipped her finger into the congealed remains of Ben's gravy.

Then she deftly smeared it deep inside Ann Droid's back and along Ann's shoulder blades and arms. She unscrewed a small cover at the back of Ann's knees, and dropped a few globules of the revolting gravy there, too.

"What the heck are you doing, Gracie?" said Ben. "You'll kill her!"

"No, I won't. This Danvers gravy stuff will work wonders. It's viscosity feels spot on to me. Better than any axle grease or oil I've ever come across. Look!"

Gracie had replaced the panel on Ann's back, pressed a couple of pressure pads on the back of her hand, and inspected her eyelids attentively.

The piglet was now cowering, apparently exhausted, under the staff dining table. Mr Stretch, by now breathless and bruised, grabbed it by the back legs again and lifted it out. With a final wriggle it leaped out of his grip, and shot out through an open window. It was soon seen rushing headlong across the astroturf playground in the direction of the school football pitches, still pursued by several members of the teaching staff.

"April Fool, everyone!" said Robbie, standing up and smiling broadly.

"Whatcha mean, April Fool?" sneered Roberta loudly.

"Well," said Robbie, still pleased with himself. "April Fool! I put the greased pig in the dining hall. It was my April Fool trick, and jolly good too, don't you agree? I hereby claim Ben's football tickets - I'll give them back to him, they're his anyway."

"Yeah, good one man!" said Vernon. "No one's ever put a pig in the dining hall before!"

"THAT'S NOT AN APRIL FOOL TRICK, DUMBO!" said Roberta. "An April Fool trick is when you trick someone! You make them think one thing is happening, and then you say April Fool to point out that they're wrong. You make a fool of them; you sell them a dummy, Dummy! You don't trick anyone by putting a pig in the dining hall, you just make a mess."

"Or the pig does," said Hector Vector.

"But it made a fool of Codger and Stretch," added Ben, hoping that a lobby of supporters might come round to Robbie's way of thinking and win him his tickets back.

60

"RUBBISH!" said Roberta. "You lot are as wet as a frog's armpit! You're not winning back these tickets unless you do something really surprising and spectacular! Work on it thickies, because the first of April is running out faster than that stupid pig."

"I'm sure one of us should be able to think of something," said Ann Droid, as bright as a button and fit as a fiddle.

CHAPTER EIGHT

"Good afternoon, Pulsar Remove. Open your auto-books at Chapter 1547. Hector, perhaps you would like to begin. Nice and loud, please."

The strange geometric-shaped boy nodded to Zolo, the teacher in charge of Space Technology at Black Hole, and slowly began to puff up his face. Within seconds, his triangular-shaped body had transformed into a rectangle and Hector was standing up in front of the class without even leaving his chair.

Ben looked across in admiration. "How does he do that?" he asked Vernon.

"What, you mean how does he morph himself?" Vernon replied.

"Yeah. How does he change himself into any shape he chooses. I mean, one minute he's sitting there, looking a lot like you or me, and the next he's..." Ben tried to think of the word.

"Morphed," Vernon helped his friend out. "It means he's changed shape. Something to do with the planet Algebra where his folks come from. Amazing people, man. So advanced."

Hector had begun to read: "The thermo-nuclear dynamics of the saline distillation theory proves that without doubt, there is evidence of a correlation in astral hydrology..."

"I don't think I can face this, today," Ben told Vernon. "It does my brain in at the best of times, but right now, all I can think about is those tickets."

Zolo slammed his ruler hard against the shiny steel desk with a loud crack.

"Ben Gordon. Would you care to be tested right now on Professor Heinrich's theory on saline distillation and astral hydrology?"

Ben looked up towards the purple-faced teacher. He was all right, Zolo, he could take a joke. But Ben could tell that he was in no mood for joking now.

"Easy, easy, Benny boy," Vernon whispered a warning to his best friend. "He's mad about something. His skin ain't nearly as purple as normal. Watch your step, dude."

"No, I'm not afraid not, Sir," Ben replied seriously.

"Then I suggest you stop talking and try to knuckle down to some serious study. Or perhaps you and the rest of Pulsar Remove would like to start coming in on Sundays as well as Saturdays?"

All eyes were on Ben. The class willed him not to say anything stupid.

"No, Sir. I'm very sorry, Sir. I'll pay special attention from now on."

Everyone breathed a sigh of relief.

"Very well," said Zolo. "Hector, perhaps you'd like to continue."

"Despite relatively little evidence of the mechanic failure of solar…" he began, and the door to the classroom whooshed open and Mr Grudge trundled in on his creaking roller feet.

"Do excuse me interrupting your most interesting lesson, Mr Zolo, but I was wondering if you could help me out."

"What does he want?" Gracie asked Ben. "He's being ever so smarmy."

"Up to no good, I'd say," sniffed Ann. "I don't like the look in his vision facilitators."

Grudge drew Zolo over to one side and

started to speak to him very earnestly.

"He definitely wants something," said Ben.

"Leave it to me, Mr Grudge," Zolo was saying to the cantankerous old robot as he wheezed his way out of the classroom. "There are some very bright pupils in this class. We should be able to sort things out for you."

"Oh, thank you, Mr Zolo," grovelled Grudge. "I always says to Mrs Danvers, I says, they is gentlemens and scholars on planet Zing and no mistake."

"I'm just Zolo, not Mr Zolo," the purple alien corrected Grudge patiently. "And I'm from the planet Zol, not Zing."

"Ah well, see I knew it began with Z, didn't I?" said Grudge hastily, as he shuffled out of the door.

As the auto-locker clicked firmly shut behind him, Grudge admired himself in the shiny metal door and began to chortle. Leaning forward he twirled his moustache victoriously. "What a mug!" he whispered to his reflection, and set off in the direction of the kitchens for a quick gossip with Mrs Danvers.

* * * *

The whole class stood in front of Silver Arrow, the school bus. Zolo had just broken the bad news.

"Let me get this straight," Roberta blurted. "You want us to try to try and fix this humungous heap of rust as a class Space Technology project."

"Exactly," confirmed Zolo. "Only this morning, the Head was telling me how important he thought it was that children should learn the more practical aspects of modern rocket technology. He's thinking of setting special new tests in it, so here's your chance for a spot of practice."

"Modern!" spluttered Vernon, as Zolo headed off to the staffroom for a cup of coffeen. "Man, this thing is about as modern as the pyramids of Egypt, and they're probably in better nick."

"Oh, come on," enthused Gracie who loved anything practical. "It's not that bad. It could be quite fun if we get this old crate started again, and if we do, at least we won't have to space walk home. Look on it as a useful lesson."

"Yeah - a history lesson," said Ann, kicking her foot playfully at the bus. With a loud clatter, the rear mudguard fell off and lay on the ground, sending up a huge cloud of rust and dust.

She looked at her handywork in horror.

"Whoops," she explained pulling a face. "Sorry Gracie, my foot slipped." But Gracie already had her head lodged under the bonnet.

"Can someone pass me my tool bag, please," she called out. "I suggest I work on the mechanical bits, while you lot start on the bodywork."

The members of Pulsar Remove had to agree that this was probably a good idea, so while Gracie nearly disappeared under the rusty old bus bonnet, they set to work with buckets, brushes and cloths to remove the layers of grime and moondust that had collected on the ancient vehicle, thanks to years of neglect by Grudge.

"Vern!" hissed Ben in a whisper. "I think I've got an April Fool idea coming on! Get a set of large spanners off Gracie, and follow me."

Vernon did as he was instructed and followed Ben into the old bus. They went up to the driver's seat and started work...

The whole class worked happily for the next half hour - or as happily as Pulsar Remove ever worked, but at the end of that time, Gracie emerged from the interior of the bus's engine compartment with a worried look on her face.

"What's up, Gracie?" asked Ann Droid. "This one got you foiled, eh Holmes?"

Gracie passed an oily palm across her forehead, smearing oil over her face.

"It's to do with the wretched electronic drive shafts and gearbox," she moaned. "The circuits are so primitive that even a super-powered brain like mine is having trouble!"

"Any idea when you might finish?"

68

asked Ann. "My mum would quite like me home some time in the next fortnight."

"You're going to have to be a little patient with me on this one," Gracie explained. "It's a tricky one, this is."

"Oh-oh. Here comes trouble," exclaimed Robbie suddenly. "Look who's on the warpath again."

Miss Wagstaff had appeared, pushing the Head on his familiar high-tech trolley across the playground. She was taking tiny, pigeon steps on account of the super-tight pencil skirt she was wearing. Everyone fell silent as the strange pair drew to a halt in front of the Silver Arrow.

"IS THOS THUG FOXED YIT?"

69

asked the Head, indicating the bus with his large vitreous eye.

Nobody said a word.

"WOLL I CUN STELL SEE SEATS IN THOR," he exclaimed. "FAR TOO COMFORTABUBBLE. DON'T WANT BLUCK HULL PUPIPS TORNING SUFT NOW, DO WEED, MOSS WIGSTIFF?"

Miss Wagstaff raised her eyes to the ultrasphere above her. She wasn't sure how much more she could take of this new regime.

"No, Head," she agreed. She was obviously on automatic pilot.

"WOLL GIT GRUDGE TO REMOVE ORL THE SEATS FROM THIS BOS!" the Head demanded. "I WANT THEM ITE AND I WANT THEM ITE NOW! SEATS IN SKULL BUSES IS NAMBY-PAMBIC RUBBISH!"

"Yes Head, I'll tell Grudge immediately," said Miss Wagstaff. As she and the Head set off back indoors Ann burst into tears.

"I can't take much more of this," she wept. "He was bad enough before, but he's turned into a complete monster now!"

"As soon as I get home," Vernon began, "I'm getting my name on the free transfer list. I don't care even if I have to go to the Yuri Gagarin Military Academy for the sons and daughters of people with really short hair and shiny shoes - I'm outta here!"

Everyone in Pulsar Remove agreed.

CHAPTER NINE

By the middle of that afternoon, life at Black Hole Primary was in full swing as normal. Well, normal except for one or two slightly unusual events and elements.

For instance, Mrs McTavish, the school secretary, was rather surprised when she thought she heard a dog barking in the parents' waiting room. She got up from behind her desk and went to investigate.

The room appeared to be empty, and she was just shutting the entrance hatch when she noticed a bright-green furry tail, sticking up like a lavatory brush on the other side of the coffee table.

There's only one creature at Black Hole with a small green furry tail, and that's Moggo, the robotic school cat. In fact he's green and furry all over, except for a bright orange nylon mane.

"Hello Moggo, dear. Sorry, I thought I heard a dog bark," said Mrs McTavish kindly, and shrugging her shoulders she left the room.

She was walking back down the corridor when she distinctly heard a dog bark behind her. "Woof! Woof!"

She retraced her steps, opened the waiting room door and spoke again to Moggo: "Is there a dog in here somewhere Moggo? I'm sure I just heard one bark?"

"Woof! Woof!" said Moggo.

"Oh, no!" said Mrs McTavish, putting her hands on her hips and staring down at him. "Someone's been reprogramming your voice control module again, haven't they? Meddlesome, naughty children!"

"Woof! Woof!" barked Moggo again. "Woof, April Fool! Woof!" And he shot past her and out of the room before she had a chance to reply.

Pulsar Remove, the Space Studies lesson with Zolo now over, moved on to the gym and a PE lesson with Mr Stretch. Polish on the top of the vaulting horse had caused several nasty mishaps, and grease on the ropes made them particularly difficult to climb. Only Ann Droid seemed able to

cope with the gym apparatus that
afternoon. She did impressive double back
flips on the beam and floor mat. She
managed hand springs, head stands and

triple somersaults until the other pupils' mouths fell open in admiration and respect. She even smiled at the same time - her face beaming like a synchronised swimmer who's feeling particularly pleased with herself.

"How's she doing all those things?" said Ben. "She's gone bionic!"

"Easy," said Gracie beside him. "It's that Danvers gravy in her joints. It's brilliant!"

PE was followed by a music lesson with Orchestra. It did not go as smoothly as Orchestra would have liked. For a start, when she sat down in front of her keyboard and started to play her favourite piece of Mozart, smoke billowed up from the back of the electronic machine, and a terrible stench filled the air.

"Right!" said Orchestra, the lights on the top of her head beginning to flash red and orange, always a sign of impending danger. "Which of you merry little tra-la-las has meddled with my organ?"

She lifted the instrument's lid, and fished out the smouldering remains of half a kipper from its innards.

"April Fool, Miss!" cried Hector Vector, his triangular face lit up with delight and triumph.

"Pathetic!" said Roberta, and she rolled her eyes ceiling-wards as if to say Heaven help me!

"Very funny, Hector, I don't think!" said Orchestra. "Perhaps I should remind you little song birds that there's a new regime in the school, and that the new Cosmic Curriculum demands that you all pass SNOT."

"SNOT, Miss?" said Robbie, puzzled.

"Yes, SNOT, the new Singing Notation and Orchestration Test. If you aren't up to Key Stage 6 by the end of this week the Head says you'll be here every Saturday until kingdom come!"

"Do we all have to pass, Miss?" asked Robbie.

"Yes Robbie, all of you. Why?"

"Well, Vernon is our best musician. He's brilliant! His dad's an opera singer. Vernon could pass Stage 6 easily. I thought maybe he could pass it for all of us. We've got enough trouble with Miss Calculate's RATS as it is."

"Well, I'm sure Vernon's musical achievements may well be an inspiration to the rest of you, but you've still all got to pass," said Orchestra. "Vernon? Where is Vernon?"

The class looked round. Vernon usually sat near Ben, but he wasn't there now. On Ben's left was Gracie, and on his right, Robbie.

"That's odd," said Orchestra. "Does anyone know where Vernon is? Ben?"

"No, Miss," said Ben. "He didn't say anything to me. He was with us in the last lesson, Miss. I don't know where he is now."

It was true. Ben had no idea where Vernon had gone.

CHAPTER TEN

"Cup of coffeen, Orchestra?"

Miss Wagstaff held out a cup of the caffeine-fortified coffee towards the music teacher who had just staggered into the staffroom.

"I don't suppose you have anything stronger, fiddle-de-dee?" warbled Orchestra, as she collapsed into a chair. "I hope I don't have another afternoon like that for a very long time, tiddley-pom!"

Looking round the staffroom, you could understand what she meant. It looked less like a teachers' meeting room and more like a battlefield at the end of a very bad day. The teachers were trying their best to recover from the blitz of pranks and practical jokes and were looking much the worse for wear. They swapped their stories of heroism and sheer guts in the face of continuous bombardment.

"I don't know," Miss Fluffety was saying to Miss Wagstaff. "Much as I admire the Head, and respect him of course, one can't help feeling he's got a little carried away with these new disciplinary measures."

Miss Fluffety dunked her digestive into her coffeen and took a large bite.

"I mean, I'm all for discipline, I always have been, but my pupils are only five years old. I do wonder if the Head isn't being a little hasty on this one."

Miss Wagstaff nodded sympathetically.

"I couldn't agree more, Fenella," she said. "Just take a look around this room. I'm not sure that everyone is capable of supporting the Head's new regime. We're not exactly a crack brigade of front-line troops, are we?"

Miss Fluffety followed Miss Wagstaff's eye to the corner where Dr Codger was sneaking a large shot of whisky into his cup of coffeen. Absent-mindedly he removed a box of chalks from the pocket of his tweed jacket, took a stick out of the packet and tried to light it. He smoked half of it before he even noticed.

"I see what you mean," Miss Fluffety agreed. "Some of the older members of staff seem to be quite shell-shocked by today's turn of events."

Miss Wagstaff was just about to help herself to another chocolate-coated-custard-cream-filled Space Nob when something outside the staff room window caught her eye. It was Grudge, scurrying across the playground towards the school garage with a large saucepan in his hand. He was moving carefully in order to prevent anything spilling from the pan, but he was obviously in a hurry. He kept glancing over his shoulder towards the kitchen.

I'm sure that crafty old rust bucket is up to something, Miss Wagstaff thought to herself.

"Tell me, are you in favour of all this testing, Miss Wagstaff?"

Mr Stretch had sauntered over to the Deputy Head and was standing in front of her with one hand on his hip, while he ran the other casually through his hair. Oh, he loves himself, thought Miss Wagstaff. There's as much space between his ears as there is between here and the other side of Mars.

"If you have any complaints about the testing system, I suggest you address them to the Head personally," Miss Wagstaff replied tartly. "I'm afraid I'm not responsible for his decisions."

"But just think of the paperwork," Miss Calculate joined in. "I already spend most of my weekends marking. What happens when we have to come in on Saturdays as well? It doesn't seem fair."

"It's not as though we're getting paid any extra," Mr Stretch added, flexing his muscles and admiring his pectorals in the mirror.

"I'm sorry, everyone, but I really have nothing more to add," Miss Wagstaff repeated. "I didn't make these decisions and to tell you the truth, I'm no happier about this reign of terror than the rest of you." Miss Wagstaff adjusted one of her extra-long dangly earrings nervously. She wished they'd all leave her alone.

"Then why don"t you do something about it?" rasped Dr Codger. "All this talk - it's action we need."

And just as he said the word action, the loudest siren you have ever heard in your life let out a massive wailing noise that shook the whole school. It was the sort of noise that makes your ears throb and your heart beat faster. The sort of noise that sent a shiver of fear down the spine of every person in the school, teachers and pupils, humans, droids and aliens alike.

The digital message screen above the staffroom door informed the teachers that their worst nightmare had just come true.

"BLACK HOLE RED ALERT! BLACK HOLE RED ALERT! THIS IS NOT A PRACTICE!"

"Oh, my goodness!" cried Miss Wagstaff, dropping her cup and jumping into action. "Quick! Let's get going."

The bright red light from the screen

flashed across their faces in time with the siren's intermittent screeching. Miss Wagstaff took charge.

"Orchestra, you go and fetch the Head immediately; he'll need wheeling into the playground. Mr Stretch, you round up the pupils, and Miss Fluffety, you'd better help him. Zolo and Miss Calculate, you come with me, the rest of you can meet us in front of the school. Let's just hope that we're not too late for whoever's fallen into that horrible hole."

CHAPTER ELEVEN

Betty Gordon, Ben's mum, went off to work that morning as normal. It was a fairly uneventful day, beginning with a parade of all the wardens, and an inspection by their leader and task master, Sergeant Major Daft-Vader.

He shouted at them (he always did that), and then he checked that their uniforms were clean and their boots were nice and shiny.

"Right you 'orrible lot!" he bellowed. "You all know what your duties are. Your job is to patrol this 'ere black 'ole and make sure no idiot goes and falls down it. If anyone does they will be sucked to an instant death in everlasting outer darkness, and you will forfeit five days' pay and a week's 'oliday. Get what I'm talking about?!"

The Black Hole Patrol Wardens, standing in their straight lines, all nodded to indicate that they had indeed got what he was talking about.

"Good!" snapped the Sergeant Major, and he sent them off on patrol, walking round and round the huge force field fence that protected the unwary from one of the largest and most vicious black holes in the entire cosmos.

Betty Gordon had been on patrol in the middle of the day, and so it was almost mid-afternoon by the time she got to the wardens' rest capsule and unpacked her sandwich lunch. Her friends Gloria Bagnold and Bob Stroud (the man who'd won the cup final tickets) were on the same shift as her, and so the three of them chatted as they munched.

"My Ben was thrilled with those football tickets, Bob," said Betty.

"So he should be, they're as scarce as hens' teeth. Gold dust apparently, if you like football, that is!" laughed Bob.

"I never really cared much for football," said Gloria. "All the swearing and spitting, arguing and kicking, and that's just in the crowd waiting to get in!"

They laughed. But they didn't laugh for long because all of a sudden the one noise that every Black Hole Warden dreads split the afternoon air. It was the wailing, deafening whine of the Black Hole Alert Siren.

WHHAAARRR! WWHHEEE! WWHHAARRR! WWHHEEEEEEE!

Almost the moment the siren started, Sergeant Major Daft-Vader smashed through the door of the wardens' capsule.

"RED ALERT, RED ALERT, RED ALERT! GIT OUTSIDE YOU 'ORRIBLE LOT! YOU'RE NOT ON A BLOOMIN' PICNIC!"

Betty, Bob and Gloria pulled on their caps and tumbled out on to the parade ground, in a flurry of uneaten sandwiches and crisps.

When they got there, the siren seemed even louder, and the pale afternoon sunshine was perforated with blue and red flashing lights from the tops of posts around the force field fence.

Suddenly a voice from a loudspeaker on a high tower, crackled into action.

"RED ALERT. BLACK HOLE VICTIM IN SECTOR NINE WEST, ALL WARDENS TO SECTION NINE WEST IMMEDIATELY."

Sergeant Major Daft-Vader, his clipboard tucked under his arm, and his mighty black boots pounding the dusty ground, led the charge towards Section Nine West.

Within moments they were going into their Black Hole Rescue Drill, speaking urgently into hand-held telephones, and hurling rope ladders, grappling irons, and long webbing tapes over the fence between the two posts where the lights were flashing at double speed. Two large lorries, with what looked like massive satellite dishes on the tops of them, were backing up and focusing magno-positive laser rays towards the hole, in a vain attempt to counteract its mighty, all-consuming suction.

"BACK EM UP. ONE TWO, ONE TWO. CHOP-CHOP!" shouted Daft-Vader. "COME ON! WE'RE NOT DEALING WITH GRANNY'S VACUUM CLEANER 'ERE!"

From the direction of the school, there approached a large and urgent posse of staff and pupils. Miss Wagstaff was in the lead, pushing the Head in front of her on his sinister high-tech trolley. Behind her were Mr Stretch, Dr Codger (not on his bicycle this time), Orchestra, Mrs McTavish, Miss Calculate, Miss Fluffety and Zolo. Then came the pupils of Pulsar Remove and the other classes.

When the Black Hole Red Alert had sounded, Ben and his friends had been enjoying break outside in the playground (you always had to go outside in break at Black Hole, unless it was wet or there was danger from a storm of comets or meteorites). They knew the drill, however. The moment the sirens started you had to stop whatever you were doing and head for the Hole. You had to report there, to be of assistance in any way you could. However chaotic, hopeless and undisciplined the pupils of Black Hole Primary might be, this reaction was burned into their consciousness. It became an automatic response, as natural to them as saying YES when someone said "Want some gum?"

Miss Wagstaff, wheeling the gruesome Head in front of her, made straight for Sergeant Major Daft-Vader.

"PLEASE GIVE ME YOUR REPORTIP. ASAPIP!" bellowed the Head.

"YES SAR!" shouted back Sergeant Major Daft-Vader. It was like two very angry dinosaurs roaring at each other across a particularly echoey piece of swamp.

"It seems, SAR!" yelled the Sergeant Major, standing to attention with his clipboard under his arm, "that a victim has fallen into the Black Hole. We have seen evidence of a human shape on our security video monitors, but as yet have located no trace of any casualty, SAR!"

"I SEEK!" said the Head.

"Do you think you'll find anyone, Sergeant?" asked Miss Wagstaff, who was now surrounded by the concerned faces of both staff and pupils.

"I don't know!" said the Sergeant Major, rather impatiently. "Once over that there fence, most victims is sucked to an instant death and lost in the innermost depths of outer darkness. They join the mysterious infinity of space, Madam," he added, by way of explanation.

"NEGATIVE VICTIM CONTACT SARGE," said the voice from the loudspeaker tower.

"It doesn't look good, Sergeant Major, does it?" suggested Mrs McTavish.

"I'm afraid not, Madam," said Daft-Vader.

The wardens had stopped throwing ropes and grappling irons, and the generators on the two large lorries cut their engines.

A deep silence filled the whole scene. Miss Fluffety dabbed the corner of her eye with a small lace hanky. The pupils round her gazed in silence at the blank face of the cruel, bleak fencing.

"I'm sorry, children," said Miss Wagstaff, her voice cracking with emotion. "But it seems that the terrible Black Hole has claimed another victim."

"APRIL FOOL!" said a loud voice

suddenly, and Vernon emerged, grinning, from behind a small tree in front of the force-field fence.

"What the...?" said Sergeant Major Daft-Vader.

"Hi, guys!" said Vernon, still beaming a broad smile. "April Fool - know what I mean?!"

A ripple of amazement ran through the assembled crowd, and especially through the pupils of Pulsar Remove.

"Do you mean, Vernon," said Miss Wagstaff in her crossest voice, "that you have fooled us into thinking that someone had fallen into the Black Hole, causing a Red Alert, setting off the alarms and mobilising all these wardens and the whole school?"

"You got it, Miss Wagstaff," said Vernon quietly, beginning to sense that she and the other adults present didn't quite share his sense of humour.

"RIGHT!" bellowed the Head suddenly. "IMMEDIAP SCHOOL ASSEMBLIDGE! NOW! IN THE HALL! BIG TROUBUBBLE!"

CHAPTER TWELVE

Only two people at Black Hole Primary had ignored the Red Alert sirens, and the first of them was Mrs Danvers. She had heard it go off all right, but she couldn't be bothered to join in the emergency.

"It'll only be some bloomin' kid who's been sucked into outer darkness," she mumbled to herself, as she did her best to get the remains of burnt liver off a pan with a hammer and chisel. "Serves 'em right for not eating up all this scrummy old liver and special gravy!"

She stood up straight to stretch her back. As she did so she realised that something in the kitchen was missing. Where was the pan full of cold gravy? Mrs Danvers was inclined to get as angry as a rhino with hornache if someone nicked her saucepans.

"Where the blin...?" she began, but

never finished her sentence, because at that moment the second person who had ignored the Red Alert emergency walked in through the kitchen door. It was her old friend and partner in moaning, Grudge.

"Here Mr Grudge," she said. "Some blighter's gone off with my best saucepan - the big black rusty one that I made that special gravy in. I've got a good mind to..."

But she didn't finish this sentence because Grudge had the big black rusty saucepan in his hand.

"Mr Grudge! Where the big black blazes have you bin with my saucepan?" she growled. "You nicked it! And I thought you was a gentleman and my friend!"

"I never nicked it, Mrs D!" said Grudge. "I borrowed it."

"Borrowed it? What for?"

"For the gravy of course - and it was excellent!"

Mrs Danvers' anger subsided as fast as a balloon with a pin in it. No one in living memory had ever complimented her on any aspect of her cooking before (except a school inspector who liked a Dead Rat Birthday Cake he mistakenly thought she'd made).

"Oh…Grudge, how very kind of you," she said, smiling. (Mrs Danvers was not a pretty sight when not smiling, but smiling didn't make her look any better.)

"I'm so glad you enjoyed it," she continued. "It should have tasted good. There was over ten kilos of lard in that there gravy!"

"I never said it *tasted* excellent," said Grudge, "and as a lower form of robotic life I can't taste anything anyway. I said it *was* excellent."

"Excellent? What for?" asked the cook, mystified.

"For mending the school bus, that's what!" said Grudge, grinning under his nicotine-coloured moustache.

"YOU WHAT?!" snarled Mrs Danvers. Her angry-as-a-rhino-with-hornache-mood was suddenly returning.

"Well, Silver Arrow, the school bus, has been playing up. I told you this morning what a wreck it is. When the Head told me to fix it up I went and saw old Zolo, and he put the kids in Pulsar Remove on to it."

"Bloomin' kids," interjected Mrs Danvers, almost by instinct.

"Bloomin' kids, as you say," continued

the rusty caretaker. "And they did it up for me, except that they couldn't fix the fact that something's gone in the main bearings in the electronic differential gearbox, or the half-shafts or summat. But I've fixed that myself! I've just tipped four litres of your cold gravy into the gearbox, and now she's going like a treat! I just started her up and revved the engine - she'll pull away from traffic lights like a cheetah what's sat on a six inch drawing pin, now!" He smiled at her.

She almost smiled back at him (still not a pretty sight).

"You mean my gravy did the trick?"

"Did the trick? It's a marvel! The best industrial-lubricant-rocket-fuel-clutch-fluid that I've ever come across! It's the greasiest grease, with added grease, in the cosmos. Why, that stuff could revolutionise the future of space travel and inter-stellar heavy haulage as we know it!"

"Oh Mr Grudge, you are kind," said Mrs Danvers. She started to blush.

Through the kitchen window the two of them could now see the staff and children returning from the Black Hole. Miss Wagstaff was in the lead, pushing the

Head in front of her on his trolley. They noticed that there was steam rising from the wobbly grey jelly that constituted his brain.

"The boss is steamed up about summat," remarked Grudge. "Tell you what, the siren's stopped and it looks like they're all heading for the school hall. Why don't you forget all that washing-up and I'll give you a lift home in Silver Arrow!"

"Would you, really?"

"Yeah, why not. They won't need me for the school run for at least twenty minutes, and with Silver Arrow's new high performance, I'll easily get you to your place and back before then."

"Well, I don't mind if I do!" said the school cook defiantly. "I've had enough of this blinkin' school for one day. Very kind of you, Grudge."

She untied her large, filthy pinny and hung it on the hook on the back of the kitchen entry hatch. She turned several large wheel valves that shut down the nuclear power to the kitchen stoves for the night, and she padlocked the fridge. "Don't want any kids coming in and nicking me cold liver slices!" she said firmly, though there was about as much chance of that as there was of Dr Codger bungee-jumping off the roof of a Mere Space Station.

The two of them slipped out through the school back door, sidled past the dustbins, and were surprised at how quiet the school was; there wasn't a single pupil or nosey member of staff in sight.

When they got to the garage Grudge slid the doors back. The late afternoon sunlight shone on Silver Arrow's elderly nose cone as Grudge helped Mrs Danvers through the passenger door and then went round to the driver's door and let himself in.

"I'm afraid you'll have to stand all the way Mrs D. The Head made me take all the seats out. He said sitting down was turning the kids into softies."

"Bloomin' kids," repeated Mrs Danvers. And she stood at Grudge's shoulder as he fired the engines into life.

With a mighty roar and large clouds of black and grey smoke, the bus edged forwards.

"Hold on to your hat Mrs Danvers, off we go!" shouted Grudge above the din, and putting his foot full on the throttle, and easing off the large handbrake, he began to show his friend what the rejuvenated school bus could do.

They shot past the bike sheds and out along the drive before you could say Moon Buggy.

"Doesn't she go well?" shouted Grudge proudly.

"Eh, yes," said Mrs Danvers, doing her best to stay upright. "I must say I wouldn't want to have to stand up all the way for a very long journey. It's very jolty!"

Grudge turned right at the lights on to Interstellar Highway 6, went down past the Astra cinema and headed out on the dual carriageway towards Orion Garden Suburb where Mrs Danvers lived.

He was just turning left into Helen Sharman Avenue when something unfortunate and unexpected happened…

CHAPTER THIRTEEN

"You realise what this means?" said Miss Calculate to a clutch of Black Hole teachers as they stepped out through the staffroom entrance hatch and turned towards the school hall and the special emergency school assembly. "He'll go and announce Saturday school. I know he will."

"I fear so, too," said Dr Codger sadly. "I dread it. When am I going to do my shopping? I was hoping to cycle down to Saturnbury's, if my bike's mended by then, that is!"

"Well, if he makes us work on Saturday," chipped in Mr Stretch, "bang goes my afternoon watching the Space Cup Final on the tele-viewer. I was really looking forward to it." (Indeed he had been. Mr Stretch was one of Lunarpool's biggest fans, and he'd bought extra beer just for the match.)

"It's all most distressing," said Miss Fluffety. "I love teaching, but not when you have to test all the under sevens and work on Saturdays."

Miss Fluffety sounded as if she was going to cry, and she wasn't the only one. The infant Venusian who hadn't eaten his gravy in Chapter Six still looked as though he was about to burst into tears. He was at the front of the queue of pupils waiting in line to go into the hall, and all round him the message was: "WE'RE IN BIG TROUBLE".

Nearer the back of the queue stood Ben, Vernon, and the other children from Pulsar Remove.

"We're for it now," said Robbie despondently. "We'll be lucky to come out of this assembly alive!"

"We've got as much chance of survival as a multi-coloured talking frog in a laser-powered liquidiser," agreed Hector Vector.

"Not funny," said the talking frog from Saturn. "Froggist, and not funny."

"Why don't you lot shut up!" It was Roberta. "All you do is moan. What's wrong with a bit of Saturday school? Honestly, you're such a bunch of wimps. You stand around like something off a knitting pattern that's been left in a ditch."

"I wish I had been left in a ditch," said the talking frog, sadly.

"Now listen up, Roberta!" said Vernon suddenly and with anger in his voice. "You challenged us to do something really, really impressive for an April Fool. You said we had to take people by surprise. What do you think I did with that there Black Hole Red Alert?"

"Yeah, he's right," said Ben, sticking up for his friend. Several other children murmured in agreement.

"Vernon may have landed us up to our armpits in nuclear waste," continued Ben, "but you can't fault him on bravery or not rising to a challenge."

"OK, OK, I admit it," said Roberta. "He may be stupid but he's got bottle."

"In fact," said Ben, pressing home the advantage, "I reckon you owe us our football tickets back. After all, Vernon's trick brought the whole school to a grinding halt. He fooled everyone, including the Head, all the staff *and* Daft-Vader and the patrol wardens!"

"Ben's right," said Robbie bravely, though he knew that crossing his twin sister at school lead to extra trouble for him when he got home.

"All right, all right," said Roberta, holding up her hand like a Robocop on point duty stopping traffic. "I must admit that Vernon's Red Alert was impressive. So impressive in fact that I will agree to award him the tickets."

Much to Robbie's relief, and the others' surprise, she reached inside the pocket of her school blazer and brought out the two precious Space Cup Final tickets.

"I would just like to point out, however," she sneered mockingly, as she presented them to Vernon, "that as it's

a racing certainty that the Head is about to announce Saturday school for the next ten light years, these stupid tickets are about as much use as a sticking plaster at a major nuclear melt-down! Ha!"

"She's right," said Robbie, dolefully.

The large entrance chamber doors at the back of the school hall opened and Miss Wagstaff started to let the infants in.

"Into the slaughter house, kiddoes!" said Roberta, still triumphant. "After you Mr Miracle!" she added to Vernon sarcastically.

They started to file towards the hall, Vernon leading the contingent from Pulsar Remove.

"By the way Mr Bravery-Before-Brains," whispered Roberta behind him, "How exactly did you manage to set the Red Alert off and not get your stupid great self sucked into outer darkness in the Black Hole? I thought someone had to fall over the fence before the alarms went off?"

"Easy, man," said Vernon quietly. "I threw a school coat over the fence. There's light beams and stuff on the other side. If you break them the bells go off. The coat went off into outer darkness, not me."

"Very clever!" admitted Roberta.

"Yeah, it was, wasn't it," said Vernon. "Especially as it was your coat!"

HOMEWORK

CHAPTER FOURTEEN

There was nothing Roberta could do to get Vernon back, as they were now inside the school hall, and in full view of the Black Hole Primary teachers.

Vernon's friends, particularly Ben, Gracie, Ann Droid and Robbie wanted to congratulate him on his trick with Roberta's blazer, but they realised that this was not the time to do it. As they came to a halt in their line near the back of the room, they sensed the air of tension and dread that hung over the whole school.

It was quite usual for the pupils in the school to fear an assembly. Whenever there was trouble concerning things like chewing gum, litter, bad behaviour in the back of Silver Arrow, or children not going out to break when they were supposed to, an assembly would be called, and the Head would be wheeled in, and the riot act would be read. They were used to this. But this afternoon's event was different. For a start the staff, standing in front of their chairs in a horseshoe on the school stage, looked as worried as the pupils.

When the whole school was in and the hall entrance hatches had been closed, there was an awkward moment of silence. Children shuffled, and Ben looked round to see if all the ancillary staff were in the room, too. He noticed that Grudge and Mrs Danvers were missing. The staff shuffled too. Miss Fluffety dabbed her eye with the corner of a small handkerchief, Dr Codger fiddled with a piece of chalk in the pocket of his old tweed jacket, and Mr Stretch looked up at the ceiling and dreamed about having a cigarette.

Then there was a sign of movement behind the dark curtains that skirted the back of the school stage, and they parted to allow Miss Wagstaff to enter, pushing the Head before her on his trolley.

Ben and the others noticed how scared and miserable the teachers now looked. Everyone looked at the floor while the Head cleared what would have been his throat if he'd had one.

The loudspeakers on the trolley crackled into life. You could cut the tension with a blunt chopstick. To the pupils of Pulsar Remove the whole experience felt more like being up before a firing squad than standing in a primary school assembly.

"STUND STILL AND LISTEN CAREFULIPLY" said the Head, loudly. "I HAVE ASKED MUSS WAGSTOP TO LIST SEVERIP EVENTS THAT TOOK PLACE TODAPE. SHE WULL PLEASE TO READ THUM TO YOU."

There was a bit more shuffling among the pupils of Black Hole. Nobody dared look up.

Miss Wagstaff came out from behind the Head's trolley and took up a position at the centre of the school stage. She had changed into a black outfit - long flares and off-the-shoulder cape in shimmering crepe de chine, and matching black kid gloves and hat, with black netting veil. She looked like something at a particularly dramatic and tragic funeral.

"Thank you, Headmaster," she said quietly. Ben noticed that under the small veil she was wearing black lipstick.

"Here is the list."

Every single pupil in the whole school held its breath.

"1. Dr Codger's bicycle brakes tampered with.

2. Impertinent notes added to Miss Wagstaff's haute couture outfit.

3. Flour and soot bombs deployed in Pulsar Remove.

4. A greased pig released into the dining hall.

5. Rare talking multi-coloured Saturn frog introduced into school dinners.

6. Plaster of Paris potato.

7. Moggo's miaow replaced with a bark.

8. Decayed half kipper put in school organ.

9. Gym equipment tampered with.

10. A Black Hole Red Alert falsely instigated."

Miss Wagstaff lowered the list in front of her, solemnly, like a lord high executioner who has just read out a death sentence and is now ready to get on with a bit of beheading.

"THUNK YOU, MISS WOGSTOFF," said the Head's voice. He paused while the horror and enormity of the day's deeds sank in.

"NUT ONLY THIS. BUT I HEAR

FROM YOUR TEACHIPS THAT
THERE HAS BEEN VERY LITTLE
PROGRESSY IN PASSING ANY OF
THE NEW SKULL TESTS!"

He paused.

"I THEREFORE HAVE SOMETHIP
TO SAY ABOUT SATURDAY LESSIPS
AND THE NEW REGIME I
INTRODIPPED THIS MORNICK.
AND IT IS THIS:

And the loudspeaker on the Head's horrible trolley let out the most terrible laugh.

It was the first time anyone at Black Hole Primary had ever heard the Head laugh.

And it was the last.

AUTHORS' NOTE

We told you at the end of Chapter Twelve that something unfortunate and unexpected happened to Mr Grudge and Mrs Danvers in Silver Arrow. What actually happened was this: as Grudge tried to turn left, the steering wheel came off in his hand. This was almost certainly because Ben had gone to work on the nut that held it in place in Chapter Eight as his contribution to April Fool's Day.

Grudge and Mrs Danvers therefore missed their turning, and headed straight on, towards Stratus X and Jupiter.

For all we know they're still somewhere up there…

Oh yes, and we thought you'd like to know that after extra time the result in the Space Cup Final was: ASTRON VILLA 4 - LUNAROOL 2. So the Villa team were over the moon!

The Fib
and other stories
by George Layton

I was sick of Gordon Barraclough: sick of his bullying and his shouting, and his crawling round Mr Melrose, sick of him being a good footballer and going on about my old football gear. So I told him it had belonged to my uncle, who'd scored thousands of goals – because my uncle was Bobby Charlton! That was the fib. Then Bobby Charlton turned up as the surprise celebrity to switch on the Christmas lights outside the town hall. "You're in for it now," said Gordon, "I told him you said he's your uncle." I looked up at Bobby Charlton. He looked down at me. If only the earth would open and swallow me up...

Based on George Layton's own childhood, here are ten short, funny stories that come straight to the point on many important items of adolescent life, such as school, girlfriends, football, and the problems of keeping in with your mates and getting round Mum.

£2.99

Vlad the Drac by Ann Jungman
£2.99
Paul and Judy are fed up with their holiday in Romania, until they find a baby vampire under a stone. They smuggle him into England, disguised as a souvenir, but all too soon the trouble starts.

Vlad the Drac Returns by Ann Jungman
£2.99
Vlad is on holiday in England, and he's bored. And whatever he starts out to do, poor old Vlad always ends up in a scrape – like the day he fell into a food mixer! Luckily Paul and Judy pick up the pieces.

Vlad the Drac Superstar by Ann Jungman
£2.99
Vlad comes to live with the Stones while he's starring in his first movie. Not only does he disrupt the whole film studio, but he becomes monstrously big for his boots at home.

Vlad the Drac Vampire by Ann Jungman
£2.99
As soon as Vlad hears about Paul and Judy's new baby sister, he comes to "help". To keep him out of mischief, Mum suggests that the children take him sightseeing – with disastrous, hilarious consequences.

The Third Class Genie
by Robert Leeson

Disasters were leading two–nil on Alec's disaster–triumph scorecard when he slipped into the vacant factory lot, locally known as the Tank. Ginger Wallace was hot on his heels, ready to destroy him, and Alec had escaped just in the nick of time. There were disasters awaiting him at home too, when he discovered that he would have to move out of his room and into the boxroom. And, of course, there was school...

But Alec's luck changed when he found a beer can that was still sealed, but obviously empty. Stranger still, when he held it up to his ear, he could hear a faint snoring... When Alec finally opened the mysterious can, something happened that gave triumphs a roaring and most unexpected lead.

A hilarious story for readers of ten upwards.

£2.99

Scrambled Legs
Jahnna N. Malcolm

ROCKY: *hot tempered*
MARY BUBNIK: *worst dancer ever*
GWEN: *shortsighted and sharp-tongued*
McGEE: *softball fanatic*
ZAN: *head permanently in the clouds*

Five friends at Deerfield's Academy of Dancing. What do they have in common? Nothing – except they all hate ballet!

"We Hate Ballet!"	£2.99
The Battle of the Bunheads	£2.99
Stupid Cupids	£2.99
Who Framed Mary Bubnik?	£2.99
The Lucky Stone	£2.99
Save D.A.D.	£2.99
The King and Us	£2.99
Camp Clodhopper	£2.99

Anastasia Krupnik is a totally engaging and precocious heroine, whose considerable insight and self-confidence generally keep her on top of her world, in spite of an occasional slip. By Lois Lowry.

Anastasia Krupnik
Anastasia comes to terms with having a baby brother.

Anastasia Again!
Anastasia and her family move to the suburbs and make friends with their elderly neighbour.

Anastasia, Ask Your Analyst!
Anastasia realises that the problem is herself, so she undertakes a course with Freud.

Anastasia at Your Service
Bored and broke, Anastasia decides to work as paid companion to a rich old lady and finds the job not quite what she had expected.

Anastasia has the Answers
Well, most of them! But one thing she knows she'll never master is climbing the ropes in the gym...

Anastasia on her Own
When her mother goes to California for ten days, Anastasia is left in charge of running the house.

Anastasia's Chosen Career
Anastasia feels she needs self-confidence, so enrols on a modelling course. But somehow she's not cut out to be a model.

All at £2.99

Order Form

To order direct from the publishers, just make a list of the titles you want and fill in the form below:

Name ....

Address ....

....

....

Send to: Dept 6, HarperCollins Publishers Ltd, Westerhill Road, Bishopbriggs, Glasgow G64 2QT.

Please enclose a cheque or postal order to the value of the cover price, plus:

UK & BFPO: Add £1.00 for the first book, and 25p per copy for each addition book ordered.

Overseas and Eire: Add £2.95 service charge. Books will be sent by surface mail but quotes for airmail despatch will be given on request.

A 24-hour telephone ordering service is avail-able to Visa and Access card holders: 041-772 2281